CANINE Companions

Dear Reader

As the ultimate companion animal, dogs have won the hearts of millions of people. Listen to an avid dog lover and you may hear reasons for ownership like: "I can buy any kind of collar for my pooch and he never asks, 'Is that the latest brand?'"; or "I can take my dogs for walks around the block, and they never say, 'Not this street again!'" and "If I come home tired, I instantly feel better when I see my puppy wagging its tail."

> "I LOVE MY FAMILY. THEY ALWAYS KNOW WHEN I'M HUNGRY, WHEN I NEED A WALK AND WHEN I NEED A CUDDLE!"
>
> AN AVID LOVER OF PEOPLE

I hope you enjoy reading about many clever dogs in this book: a team of mushing surveillance dogs in Greenland, the Canadian Avalanche Rescue Dogs, working border collies on farms, and Joey, a star agility sports dog who was adopted by Kelly.

P.S. My two dogs are treasures. Above is an image of me holding Soots and Bibi back from tearing off down the street!

Sharon Parsons

My sincere thanks to the following people for their time, information, images and enthusiasm for this book:

Greg Fontana and staff, Boarding School for Dogs, Victoria, Australia

Kelly Messenger and Joey, Sit Happens Dog Training, Sydney, Australia

Kyle Hale and Bruce Watt, Canadian Avalanche Rescue Dog Association, British Columbia, Canada

For learning solutions, visit cengage.com.au

Contents

CANINE Companions

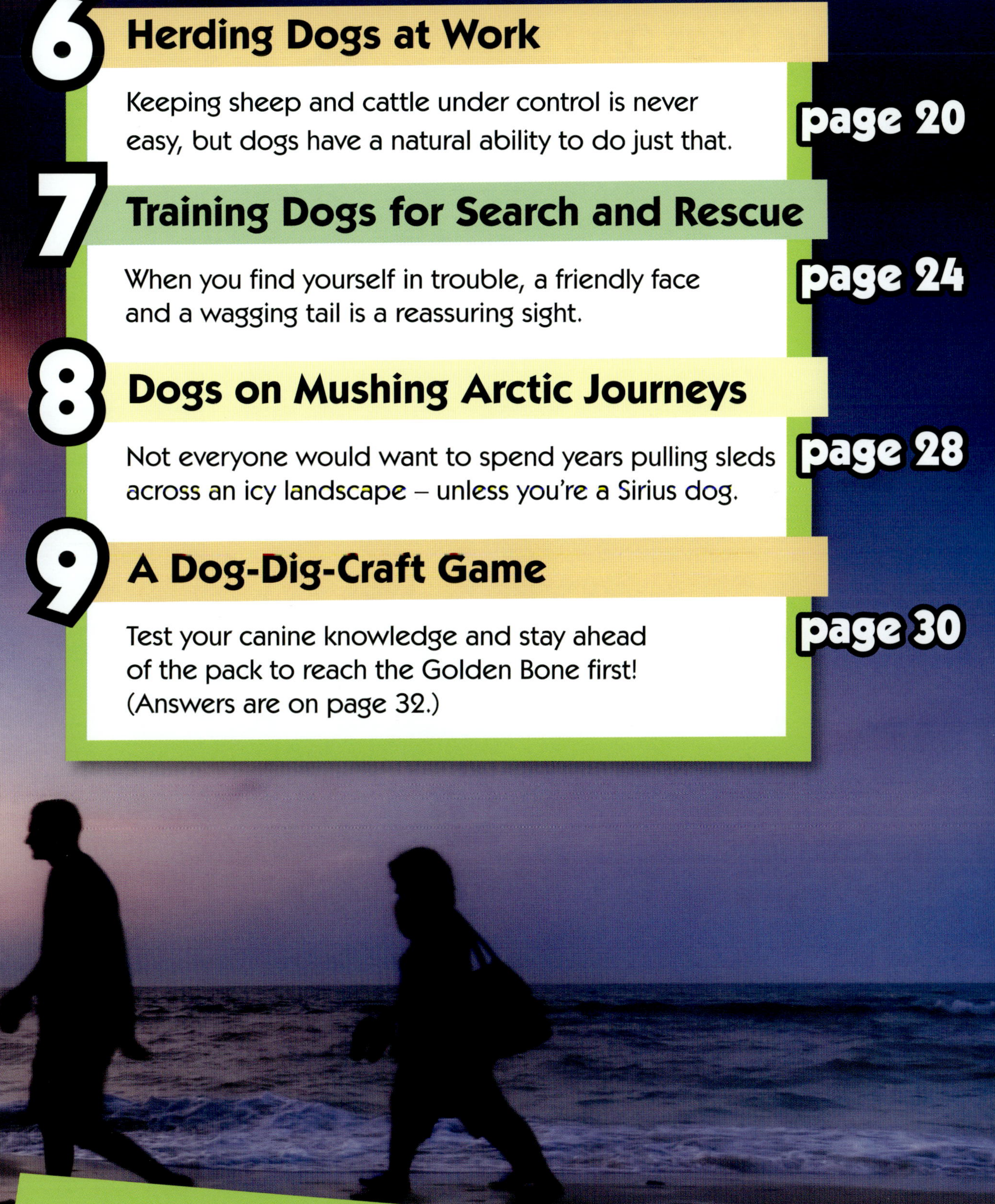

1 Are Dogs Our Friends?

Welcome to my world!

Dogs have long been revered in many cultures around the world as the ultimate animal companions for their loyalty, intelligence and adaptability as domestic pets, and also as workers. There are numerous breeds and crossbreeds in the canine world that enable people to choose which dog best suits their needs and their environment. Dogs instinctively operate as pack animals, so we have had to adapt to their natural instincts when living with them or training them for specific purposes.

Wild Canines

Not Socialised

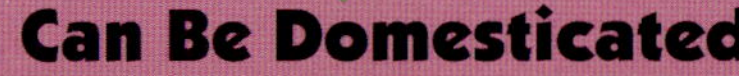

Can Be Domesticated

Can Be Socialised

Wolves

Dogs

Dingos

Wolves and dogs are closely related and their behaviours are very similar. The main difference is that for tens of thousands of years, humans have selectively bred dogs to shape their characteristics into ones that humans can live with. By selecting and breeding from generations of calmer, less aggressive dogs, humans have modified breeds that are less temperamental and easier to control. Domestic dogs are willing to accept humans as part of their pack, whereas wild dogs and wolves are not.

Some wild dogs, such as dingos, can become socialised (but never domesticated) if they are taken into a human environment before the age of eight weeks.

CAUTION: While it has taken thousands of years to shape modern domestic dogs' characteristics, it can take only a matter of months for a dog to revert to its wilder instincts. Stray or abandoned dogs often form packs to hunt and can become very aggressive.

The Psychology of Pack Behaviour

Packs in the Wild

In the wild, dogs learn to cooperate with other members of their pack from an early age. They also learn to submit to the will of the pack leader, or "alpha" dog. If they don't, they become outcasts and have little chance of survival on their own.

Packs in the Home

This characteristic makes dogs ideal for training by humans. When dogs are brought up in a domestic environment, they assume that the humans are their pack. They also identify one of the humans as the alpha dog, and will obey his or her commands. Dogs can become confused when they get commands from too many people.

Pack Territory

While pack behaviour may be useful in many situations, it can also become dangerous if people do not understand how a dog thinks. When a stranger comes to the house, for example, a dog will immediately realise the person is not a member of its pack, and it may become defensive. It will look to see if the alpha dog (its owner) accepts that person. That's because a dog regards its surroundings as its pack territory, and may become aggressive if someone from outside their pack crosses into their space.

Bark Warnings

The dog's idea of territory can also cause it to bark. Barking can serve to "call" the other members of the pack back to their territory, which is why a dog left alone may often bark constantly. Barking can also warn other non-pack-member dogs to keep away, which is why a dog may bark when it hears another dog, even if it's just walking by.

Caution for Children

In the wild, pack behaviour is based on a hierarchy. Dogs that are more aggressive and dominant are higher up in the hierarchy. The alpha dog is always at the top – but the lower-ranked dogs may fight to exert dominance over each other. This may cause problems when a dog encounters a child who is not a member of their pack. A dog's natural instinct is to try and dominate what it sees as a lower-ranked dog.

Understand and Care

Once you understand how dog psychology works, it's easy to see that extreme care should be taken around all dogs, regardless of their size, until they have clearly accepted you as part of their pack. Even then, it is important to understand that a dog will only ever see you as another dog, so don't expect it to behave like a human.

A Boarding School for Dogs

All domesticated dogs require training, preferably when they are young, to teach them how to live harmoniously with people. Otherwise, some dogs can develop behavioural problems. However, not everyone has the time or skills required to do this. Dog owners who require extensive help can send their pets to a dog-training facility. At the Boarding School for Dogs in Victoria, Australia, dogs receive training for a range of issues, including antisocial behaviour such as aggression or anxiety. This allows handlers to work consistently on dogs' behavioural problems.

Dog handlers work with the dogs in the same area to assist in their distraction training.

Aggressive Dogs

There are all kinds of behavioural problems that dog trainers are asked to correct, but the most common one is the aggression that dogs can show towards people and other animals. Usually, aggression is a behaviour that dogs exhibit when they feel nervous or upset, and this is their way of protecting themselves. A dog boarding school can implement a step-by-step approach over ten or 20 days that is tailored to each dog's breed and particular needs.

Baring teeth is a serious example of aggressive behaviour.

First Training Stage for Dogs

Develop Trust and Routines

When a new dog attends a boarding school, the handler spends time becoming acquainted with its personality traits in order to develop a working relationship built on trust and respect. Trainers build trust with their dog students by being calm, firm and consistent with their commands, rewards and methods of dog handling. Meal times are important for developing consistent routines of behaviour. Manners are also important for developing good behaviour. For example, a dog is trained to wait before running out a gate until instructed to do so. This routine establishes the human as the pack leader.

Second Training Stage for Dogs

Test Success of Training

Once a dog is consistently able to respond to commands, the trainer introduces some challenges and distractions to test if the dog can continue to exhibit the new learned behaviour. This is done by placing the dog in distraction-filled scenarios to replicate life outside the boarding school.

distraction training among many dogs

A beagle relaxes with its trainer.

Third Training Stage in the Home

Training Owners

Once a dog has successfully completed its boarding school course, it is rehabilitated, which means it exhibits more relaxed and controlled behaviour around other animals and people. A rehabilitated dog then returns home, where the trainer works with the owners to reinforce the boarding school's training principles.

Value of Professional Training

Professional dog trainers offer an essential service to dog owners because they have the expertise and experience to tailor training programs for all kinds of dogs. Their training programs help to prevent, as well as correct, socially unacceptable behaviour so that dogs and people can live together in a happier, safer and more relaxed way.

Miniature Horse Helps in Distraction Training

Result: dog can calmly sit close to animals

Before arriving at the school, the golden retriever was easily distracted around other animals, so it underwent a distraction training program assisted by the school's resident miniature horse, Simon.

Result: dog can walk past animals without distraction

The golden retriever is an intelligent dog and it quickly learnt how to walk past Simon in the school's enclosed training area.

Result: dog can lay down close to animals

After a ten-day program, this golden retriever calmly lay down beside Simon.

Before: Aggressive Boxer

When this boxer started the 20-day training program, it would not allow any animal to pass through the gate into its grassed area, or its territory.

The Test: Amazing Results

Finally, it was time to test the boxer. Simon passed by the boxer into its territory, and the boxer exhibited calm behaviour.

After: Calm, Trained Boxer

After the 20-day program, the boxer passed with flying colours! As for the miniature horse? He continues to help train some of the most problematic dogs at the school.

“WE ARE HAPPY WHEN DOG OWNERS GIVE THEIR PET DOGS AND FAMILIES A BETTER CHANCE OF LIVING TOGETHER IN A MORE FULFILLING WAY.

GREG FONTANA, FOUNDER OF THE BOARDING SCHOOL FOR DOGS”

3 Adopted Dog is a Sports Champ!

Joey is a border collie-cross-cattle dog who was born in the state of Washington in the USA. During her first six months, Joey lived with a family where she suffered some mistreatment. As a result of that experience, Joey became fearful and aggressive towards men and teenagers. Joey ended up in an animal shelter but was found by a Canadian working-dog rescue organisation and taken to Vancouver, Canada. She was placed with a kind foster family for six months.

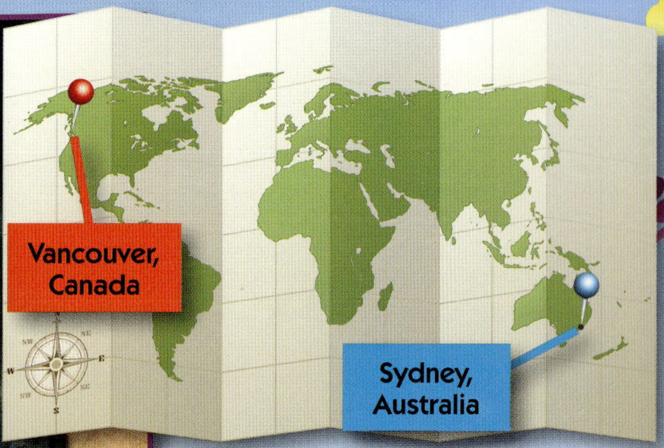

"Hey Kelly, I want that ball!"

a close-up of a relaxed Joey

Joey poses for the camera.

Kelly Adopts Joey

When Kelly met Joey at the foster home, Joey ran straight up to her for pats. When the foster family told Kelly that that was the first time Joey had done that to a stranger, Kelly knew that she was meant to adopt this dog. At that time, Joey was hyperactive, aggressive to certain people, and urinated when she was scared. Kelly enrolled herself and Joey in a dog training program, and she also introduced Joey to flyball, her first of many dog sports. Very quickly, Joey's behaviour changed and she became more confident. Kelly says that it felt great to have helped her beautiful dog.

Canine Sports Training

Kelly and Joey relocated to Sydney, Australia, in 2009, and they continued their participation in dog sports. That year, Kelly enrolled Joey in the DockDogs competition at the World Dog Games. Joey had never tried this sport before but, with only six weeks before the World Dog Games, and because Joey loves fetching balls, Kelly was able to prepare Joey for the event.

Kelly says, "A ball thrown into the water presents an extremely exciting challenge for Joey. She has learnt that the further she jumps into the water, the quicker she gets the ball, and in the arena of agility sports this translates into success!"

A World Dog Games Win

In October 2009, Joey became famous at the first ever World Dog Games, held in Australia. Joey jumped the furthest of all the dogs that entered from around Australia. The judges were impressed when Joey managed to jump 23 feet and 8 inches (about 7.2 metres) to fetch the ball. Suddenly, all the media wanted to know about Joey, the wonder dog!

Joey competes in the DockDogs competition.

The Epilogue to Joey's Story

Soon after the World Dog Games, Joey's foster "father" (who used to live in South Australia) returned to Australia to see his family, so he visited Kelly and Joey. Kelly says, "Joey hadn't seen him in over two years, but as soon as she heard his voice, she started whining excitedly and melted into a 'wiggling puddle' when he started petting her." Today, Kelly proudly says, "Joey is my little sidekick. She goes everywhere with me now because she is so well behaved. In my opinion, a well-trained dog is a free dog, and if Joey could talk, I know she would agree wholeheartedly with me."

Joey completes her jump on target.

Joey rests after fitness training at the beach, her absolute favourite place.

> "ALL IN ALL, JOEY IS LIVING PROOF THAT WITH A LITTLE TIME AND PATIENCE, EVEN THE MOST DIFFICULT AND PROBLEMATIC DOG CAN BECAME A WONDERFUL COMPANION THAT IS A JOY TO SPEND TIME WITH."
>
> KELLY MESSENGER

Joey's Flyball Event

Flyball is a competitive relay event between two teams of four dogs. Joey was the first dog in her team to jump four hurdles in the team's lane, running towards the flyball box. Once there, Joey pushes the pedal on the flyball box which releases a ball for her to retrieve, before returning over the hurdles back to the start line. The team that finishes first, without errors, wins the relay event.

Kelly gets ready to show Joey another ball to encourage her to run faster to the finish line.

Flyball Lane

The length of each flyball lane is 15.54 metres.

Flyball Hurdles

In Australia, the hurdle height is set at 12.7 centimetres lower than the shoulder of the smallest dog in the team. Each hurdle is spaced at 3.05 metres apart.

Flyball Box

The flyball box is 4.57 metres from the fourth hurdle.

Kelly is at the finish to guide Joey back to the team.

HUMANITY FEATURE

Animal Welfare

Around the world there are many people and animal welfare organisations that are dedicated to helping abandoned, neglected and stray animals, many of whom are injured or sick.

The Royal Society for the Prevention of Cruelty to Animals (RSPCA)

In Australia, the RSPCA is a charity that was first formed in Victoria in 1871, but these days it works within every Australian state and territory. The RSPCA undertakes many roles and actively campaigns at events and in the media to prevent cruelty to animals.

Their shelters provide havens for animals that have been left unwanted, sick, stray and injured – mostly dogs and cats. All animals receive veterinary care, sustenance and a safe home. Then, they undergo temperament checks and training before people can adopt any of them as pets.

World Society for the Protection of Animals

For over a quarter of a century, the World Society for the Protection of Animals (WSPA) has worked in areas of the world where limited or no animal welfare organisations exist. Their four main areas of focus are:

- companion animals e.g. the promotion of responsible pet ownership
- wildlife exploitation e.g. the prevention of cruel treatment of wild animals
- farm animals e.g. the inhumane transport of animals
- animals in disasters e.g. the care of animals suffering in human-induced or natural disasters.

RSPCA IN NEW ZEALAND

The Royal New Zealand Society for the Prevention of Cruelty to Animals (RNZSPCA) provides help to animals and owners.

Social Studies

The Lost Dogs' Home

In 1910, The Lost Dogs' Home in Melbourne began its life as one of the largest and most valued animal welfare organisations in Australia. The dedicated teams of animal helpers and veterinarians have kept the shelter's doors open for about 20 000 dogs and cats that are lost, stray or abandoned every year.

> WSPA'S VISION IS OF A WORLD WHERE ANIMAL WELFARE MATTERS, AND ANIMAL CRUELTY ENDS.
>
> WSPA

4 Canine Health

Veterinarians promote responsible dog ownership so that pets are kept healthy. Good hygiene practices in the home, combined with regular vaccinations and health checks, will reduce the risk of disease and illness in pet dogs. This vigilance will prevent diseases spreading to other dogs, and prevent humans contracting some diseases, too.

Yearly Immunisations

When acquiring a new dog, it is essential that they have an official record of their vaccinations. Both Australia and New Zealand have similar immunisation or vaccination requirements. Some immunisations that dogs must have from the time they are puppies aged six to eight weeks old are:

Canine Distemper Virus: a rare disease due to the mandatory vaccinations against it. It can spread from infected dogs to unimmunised dogs via sneezing and coughing, much like a human contracts a cold. It can affect a dog's breathing and brain function.

Canine Parvo Virus: a highly contagious disease, especially in puppies and young dogs, but older dogs can also carry the virus. This virus causes severe vomiting and diarrhoea, sometimes with fatal consequences.

Canine Infectious Hepatitis: a highly fatal virus that can affect the liver and the kidneys. Between unvaccinated dogs, this virus can spread via the faeces, saliva and urine.

Kennel Cough or Canine Cough Virus: the two viruses that cause this respiratory disease are not usually fatal. The dog makes a sound like a dry, hacking cough, as if something is stuck in its throat. The name "kennel cough" originated because it can be more easily contracted when large groups of dogs are close together at shows or in boarding kennels.

"Ouch, you said I wouldn't feel this injection!"

Q: Can people get diseases from their dogs?

A: People are unlikely to get sick when exposed to a dog's germs or illness. However, young children and people who are immunodeficient are at a higher risk of becoming ill if they are come into contact with affected animals. A measure people can take to avoid disease is to always wash their hands thoroughly after handling dogs and other animals.

Q: What is one reason why people should wash their hands after handling or cuddling puppies?

A: Puppies can pass the *Campylobacter* bacteria in their faeces, so miniscule traces may rub off on people's hands. This bacteria can cause diarrhoea when transmitted to humans.

Worms

Common worms are parasites that live inside a dog's intestines, but they can spread to the dog's vital organs, too. These worms are commonly known as "roundworms" and, among the many symptoms, they can cause vomiting and diarrhoea. It is recommended by veterinarians that dogs be given worm treatments every three months.

Fleas

Just mention the word "fleas" and you may feel the need to scratch! But in the world of dogs, fleas can cause much distress by irritating the skin, causing various health problems, and spreading disease from animal to animal. One effective method of controlling fleas in the home and on most dogs is to use flea sprays, because they usually contain pyrethrum, which is safe for mammals. But the best method of controlling fleas should be discussed with veterinarians.

PYRETHRUM

Pyrethrum is a natural insecticide that can be sourced from the flowers of certain species of chrysanthemum plants.

Heartworms

A heartworm is also a roundworm, but it lives in the right side of a dog's heart and can cause extreme tiredness. If left untreated, it can be fatal. It passes from dog to dog via a mosquito piercing the skin of its host and leaving larvae under the skin, which make their way into the dog's blood vessels and then to the heart.

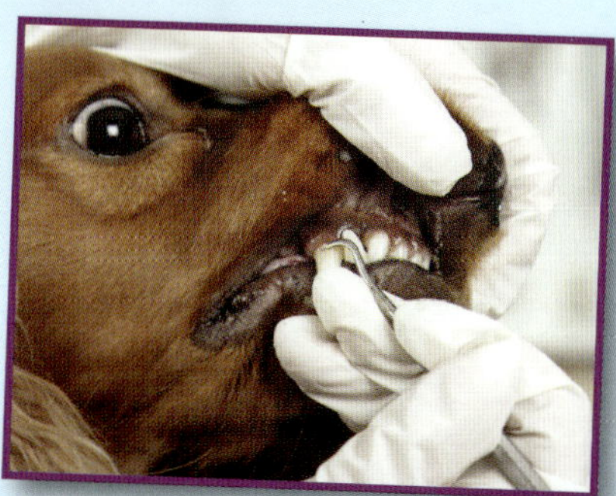

Periodontal Disease

This is a common disease in dogs as they age. Periodontal disease refers to the many diseases that affect the health of a dog's gums and teeth. A vaccination is recommended for certain dog breeds.

5 Canine Breed Categories

Pure Dog Breeds

While there are many names for categories or groups of dogs, Chapter 5 provides one grouping for pure dog breeds, and their innate features and characteristics.

CROSSBREDS

Dogs that are referred to as crossbreds have been bred from two dogs that are not of the same breed. The parents may be of different pure breeds or crossbreds.

A labradoodle is a crossbred dog – a labrador and a poodle are mated to produce labradoodle puppies.

Working Dogs

As a domestic pet, this group of working dogs needs to be exercised daily, as their breeds were traditionally used for jobs like guarding animals and pulling carts and sleds. Some dogs that belong to this breed are:

boxer, Doberman and Siberian husky.

Siberian husky

Herding Dogs

These are working dogs with natural herding abilities, who help farmers to control sheep and cattle herds by nipping at the animals' heels and staring or barking at them. Some popular herding dog breeds are:

Australian cattle dog, Australian shepherd and border collie.

"Now, where are those sheep?"

Hound Dogs

Hound dogs can use their acute sense of smell in all kinds of useful situations. One valuable role is at airports, working alongside quarantine staff. They are trained to sniff out illegal substances and items, such as food and plants, which may adversely affect the country's crops or ecosystems. Dogs categorised as hound dogs include:

beagle, Afghan hound and bloodhound.

a bloodhound at work

Sporting Dogs

In certain seasonal and recreational activities, these agile, high-energy dogs have the innate ability to work with hunters to find and retrieve animals. Dogs categorised as sporting dogs include:

golden retriever, labrador retriever.

Labradors possess a good temperament and natural traits that help when they are involved in outdoor activities and inside the family home.

Terrier Dogs

Terriers love digging, and are so-called after *terra*, the Latin word for "earth". They are indeed terrors if untrained and left unsupervised in backyards. Their natural instinct is to hunt and dig for prey such as rodents. Popular terriers include:

Scottish terrier, Maltese terrier and Jack Russell terrier.

Toy Dogs

Traditionally, these small dogs were an ideal size to hunt out rodents. However, their cute features and small size make them great companions as pets in the home, and many have adapted very well to a life of pampering! Recognise any of these toy dogs?

Shih tzu, Chihuahua, poodle (small) and cavalier King Charles spaniel.

Non-Sporting Dogs

A diverse group of dogs belong to this group as a result of their varying sizes, temperaments, coats and colours. Some of them are:

Bichon Frisé, Dalmatian, bulldog, poodle (large).

SCIENCE FEATURE

Popular Dogs

Dog ownership statistics in countries such as the UK and the USA show that highly intelligent, medium-to-large-sized dogs make the most popular pets.

labrador

Compare Top Dogs Over Ten Years

According to the American Kennel Club's dog registrations, there were some changes to the top five most popular dog breeds over a ten-year period.

2001

1 = Labrador

2 = Golden retriever

3 = German shepherd

4 = Dachshund

5 = Beagle

2011

1 = Labrador

2 = German shepherd

3 = Beagle

4 = Golden retriever

5 = Yorkshire terrier

beagle

Some Smart Dogs ... Do You Agree?

Amongst dog experts, there are certain dog breeds that consistently demonstrate high intelligence, especially in training situations.

1 = Border collie

2 = Poodle

3 = German shepherd

4 = Golden retriever

5 = Doberman pinscher

German shepherd

poodle

6 Herding Dogs at Work

Australian cattle dog

Certain canine breeds have an innate ability to herd animals (any animals, even their owners, if they could!) in any environment. Around the world, these clever canines have adapted to, or have been specially bred to, sustain the extremes of their climate and rigours of the farming terrain.

Breeding for the Environment

In Australia, the Australian cattle dog was bred to work in the country's hot, dry outback climate. While the dog's complete breeding history is still not clear, it is understood that British settlers in the 1800s crossbred their sheep-herding dogs with local breeds, such as the dingo. One example is when Thomas Hall imported the blue smooth Highland collie and crossbred it with a dingo. The breed became known as the Hall's heeler (and later the blue heeler) because it had a blueish coat and nipped the cattle's heels when herding them.

blue smooth Highland collie + dingo = blue heeler

Australian Cattle Dog Today

Today, the Australian cattle dog is not only a great companion, it has demonstrated its intelligence and problem-solving skills when working with livestock, and its adaptability in Australia's diverse environments and climates.

Original Breed Standard for the Australian Cattle Dog

In 1902, Robert Kaleski prepared a breed standard, listing the physical features that he believed an Australian cattle dog should have. Part of that breed standard is below.

DOG BREED STANDARD

A dog breed standard is also known as a "bench standard". It is a document that describes the ideal physical and behavioural features of dogs belonging to a particular breed. People at dog-breeding clubs usually write breed standards, and they can vary from club to club. They are a useful checklist for judges at dog shows.

Shoulders: strong with good slope for free action **7 points**

Head: broad between the ears, tapering to a point at muzzle **15 points**

Height: about 20 inches; bitches a little smaller **7 points**

Back: straight, with ribs well sprung, ribbed up **7 points**

Ears: short and pricked, running to a point at tip **10 points**

Hindquarters: strong and muscular **12 points**

Eyes: brown, quick and sly looking **7 points**

Chest: deep, but not out of proportion to body **7 points**

Feet: small and cat shaped **7 points**

Legs: great muscular development **7 points**

Coat: short, smooth and very dense **7 points**

Colour: head: black or red; body: dark blue on back; lighter blue, sometimes mottled with white hairs on underpart of body **7 points**

TOTAL = 100 points

Australian Shepherd at Rest

The Australian Shepherd is an agile and muscular breed that can work for a whole day, herding sheep in all kinds of conditions. It appears to have been bred from a European herding dog and a border collie.

The Stare of the Border Collie

As amazing as it may appear to onlookers, border collies use their stare to herd many kinds of animals for farmers! It is known as "the eye," and, by directly staring at the animals, border collies can intimidate them to move in the direction that they want them to go. Traditionally, working border collies herd sheep and cattle. But these instinctively clever dogs can also herd free-range chickens, pigs and even ostriches!

In New Zealand, a border collie gives "the eye" to a flock of sheep.

Whistle Commands for Working Border Collies

Working border collies can be trained very quickly to herd livestock, either by responding to the farmer's voice commands or certain sound commands of a multitone whistle.

The popular half-moon-shaped whistle has a higher-frequency sound than the human voice and can be heard by the dog from a great distance.

A farmer uses the whistle to command the border collies.

Communication

Whistle Commands

Whistle commands are a form of communication between a farmer and his or her dog. When herding sheep, a farmer can instruct a border collie to do what is required to herd stock into the desired area. A different whistle sound is used instead of a voice command, and some are:

- *"lie down" or "stop"(a long whistle sound)*
- *"walk up" (two short whistles): tells the dog to walk up to the livestock*
- *"come by" (wheet-wheeo sound): communicates to the dog to move around the stock in a clockwise direction*
- *"way to me" (whee-who sound): instructs the dog to move around the stock in an anti-clockwise direction*
- *"take time" (hee-hee-hee-hee sound): short whistle sounds in quick succession to slow down the dog to a steady pace.*

Sheepdog Trials

In 1873, sheepdog trials were first recorded in Wales, UK. They were originally intended as a way to identify the best working dogs to herd livestock together. But this tradition has developed over the years into sporting competitions around the world, too. The border collie's amazing herding talents and ability to learn quickly has also enabled it to compete in other sports, such as flyball and disc dog competitions.

The border collie has a worldwide reputation as the ultimate sheep-herding dog in sheepdog trials for its intelligence, stamina, alertness and agility.

a rottweiller

Tracking Trials

Tracking trial competitions offer the olfactory senses of many dog breeds (including border collies, Rottweilers, German shepherds and cavalier King Charles spaniels) to find a "lost person" or item in a controlled territory. Each dog is assessed to determine which dog was the best performer on the day.

Disc Dog Competitions

Judges in disc dog competitions provide scores to dogs when they catch a thrown disc before it lands on the ground. If a dog can catch a disc in mid-air with all four paws on the ground, it gains an extra half-point.

A round disc is thrown into the air for the dog to catch.

7 Training Dogs for Search and Rescue

Often we have witnessed inspiring stories of search and rescue that were only made possible with the help of specially trained dogs. The natural loyalty of dogs towards their owners, as well as their intelligence and innate senses, have proven invaluable at times when people have relied on their support.

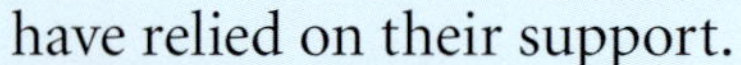

At Airports

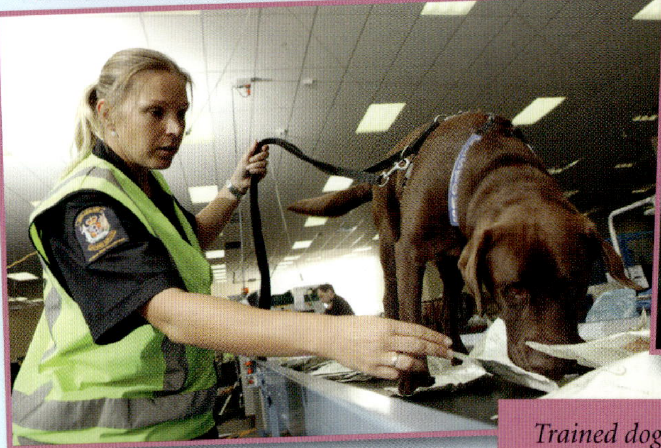

Trained dogs help quarantine staff by sniffing out illegal items in passenger luggage.

At Mines

If parts of a mine collapse, dogs can sniff out and alert rescue workers, where miners are located.

In Natural Disasters

Earth can be a volatile environment, and when natural disasters occur, the instincts of specially trained dogs provide beneficial support for search and rescue workers.

Training Purebred Dogs for Search and Rescue

Certain breeds of dogs can be trained for search-and-rescue work, but their training needs differ to those used for domestic pets. Dog training experts suggest that purebred dogs are easier to train becase they exhibit more predictable behaviour than crossbred dogs. Some tips to get started are below.

- choose a purebred: German shepherd, border collie, labrador, golden retriever
- enrol in a puppy training program at a specialised dog training school
- spend a lot of time to develop a strong bond
- discourage chasing animals
- reward settled and focused behaviour
- supervise structured activities
- control socialisation with people and animals

Canadian Avalanche Rescue Dogs

The Canadian Avalanche Rescue Dog Association (CARDA) is a not-for-profit organisation that is entrusted to train and maintain a network of search-and-rescue services in Canada's avalanche-prone areas. The handlers and their dogs are a highly trained and skilled team that are dedicated to saving lives in high-risk areas.

ready to start searching in the dangerous avalanche zone

looking out from the helicopter

waiting for a helicopter to air lift them from the avalanche site

A Snapshot of CARDA's Work

In 1978, two snow patrollers were trapped in an avalanche on Whistler Mountain in Canada. Once rescued, one of the patrollers (Bruce Watt) began the research and training that led him to form CARDA in 1982. In December 2000, a CARDA team member and his dog Keno made the first successful live rescue in Canadian history.

Bruce Watt with his avalanche rescue dog, Radar

Avalanches

Avalanches can be caused by the effects of changeable weather and by people disturbing the snow on mountain slopes.

Main Causes of Avalanches

Steep Slope

Unstable Snow

Changeable Weather

A combination of two or more factors can cause avalanches. Slopes that have a gradient of 25 per cent or more are prone to avalanches, and skiers and snowboarders tend to ski on slopes with a gradient of 30 to 40 per cent. Each of these factors can lead to unstable snow.

a welcome sight for avalanche survivors

Canada

Canada boasts some magnificent mountainous areas and during the snow season, between November and March, people are drawn to the area's beauty, adventure and challenge. In this majestic yet fragile environment, people do all kinds of activities, such as snowmobiling, downhill skiing, snowboarding, snowshoeing, backcountry (cross-country) skiing, hiking and climbing. The Canadian road and rail system also winds its way through snow-covered, mountainous areas so avalanches are a potential hazard for people who travel through Canada, too.

8 Dogs on Mushing Arctic Journeys

Mushing is an adventure sport or a means of transport that relies on a team of dogs to pull a sled. As a sport, mushing is popular in North America and Northern Europe.

Serious Sirius Mushing Surveillance

Greenland is the world's largest continental island with the world's largest national park. This region is under Denmark's rule, and every five years the military dogsled team patrol about 8 000 kilometres of the northeast coastline.

The military operation is called "Sirius". The Sirius dogs work for five years only, and by the end of their working life may have travelled in the sled team for about 20 000 kilometres. It is mushing at its most adventurous! The team of specially bred dogs, led by their patrol companions, travel across a white, rugged landscape in a treacherous, below-zero climate for two years. They travel under the constant threat of potential injuries from environmental dangers, as well as from polar bear attacks.

a Sirius husky at rest

Sirius patrollers and their dogs are on the job.

Physical Science

Sirius

Sirius is also the name given to the brightest star in the night sky (which is actually two stars, circling each other closely). Its common name is the "dog star", as it forms part of the constellation called "Canis Major" (or the "Great Dog").

9 A Dog-Dig-Craft Game

Objective

To play this game, you will need to answer questions about the information that you have read in each chapter of this book. You can either play the game on these pages or design your own version on a large sheet of cardboard.

Game Materials

- **Player 1** makes six tiny, red, bone-shaped counters to fit into each section of this game. Use cardboard or paper.
- **Player 2** makes six tiny, blue, bone-shaped counters to fit into each section of this game. Use cardboard or paper.
- two plastic counters
- one die.

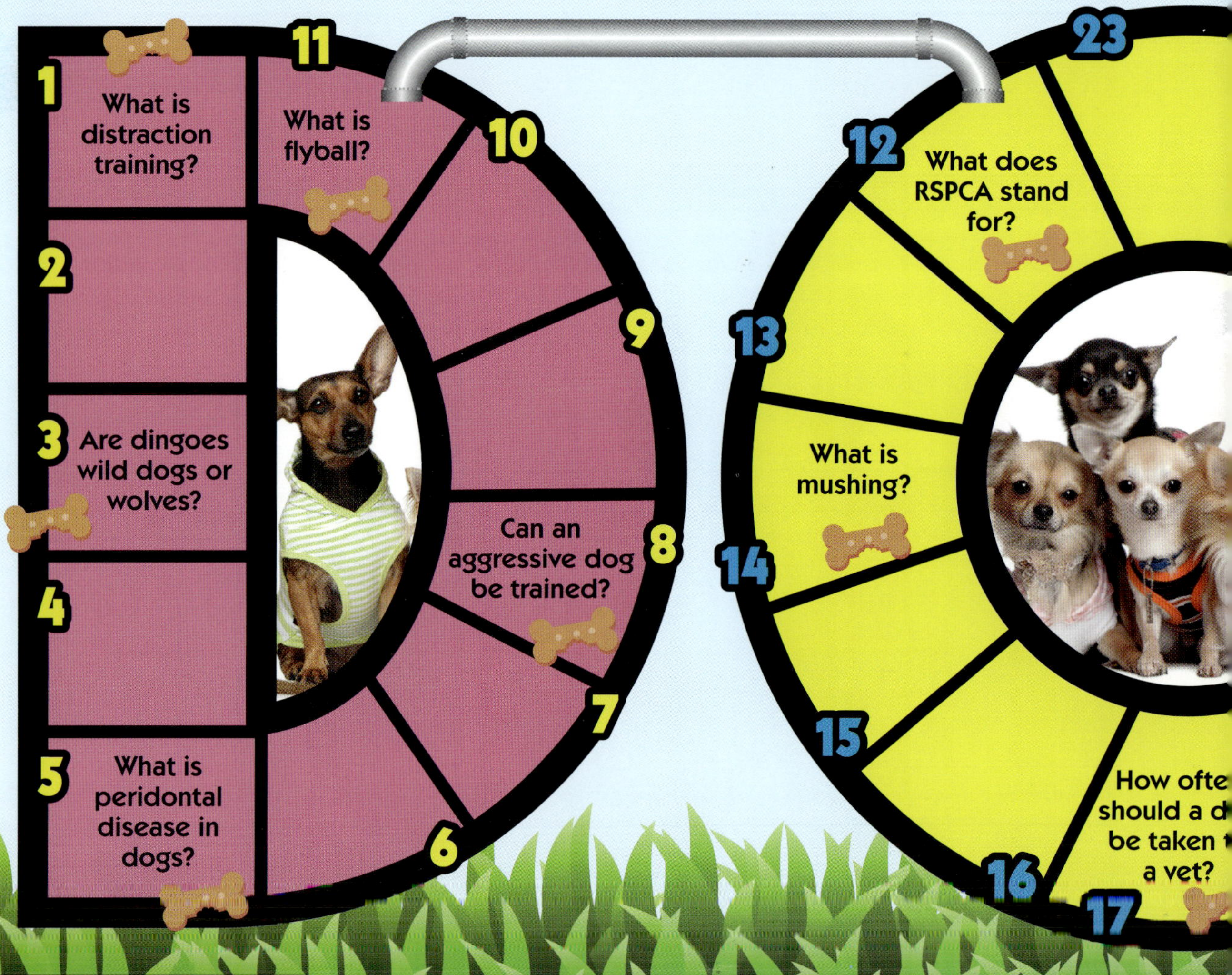

1 What is distraction training?

2

3 Are dingoes wild dogs or wolves?

4

5 What is peridontal disease in dogs?

6

7

8 Can an aggressive dog be trained?

9

10

11 What is flyball?

12 What does RSPCA stand for?

13

14 What is mushing?

15

16

17 How ofte should a d be taken a vet?

23

Rules of Play

Player 1: Begins with six red, bone-shaped counters, plus one plastic counter.

Player 2: Begins with six blue, bone-shaped counters, plus one plastic counter.

Play the Game: Each player takes their turn to throw the dice and count along the series of tunnels and shafts – there are bones at different points and levels. When a player lands on a bone, they cannot place their bone counter on the game's bone unless they answer the question correctly.

And the Winner Is: The player who reaches the "Golden Bone" first and has covered the most game bones with their coloured bone counters … wins the game. But, if a player with fewer bones reaches the "Golden Bone" first, that player can still win if they can answer the bonus question correctly.

Bonus Question: Which dog breeds are considered to be the most popular and most intelligent?

Game Answers: The page numbers for the game's answers are on page 32.

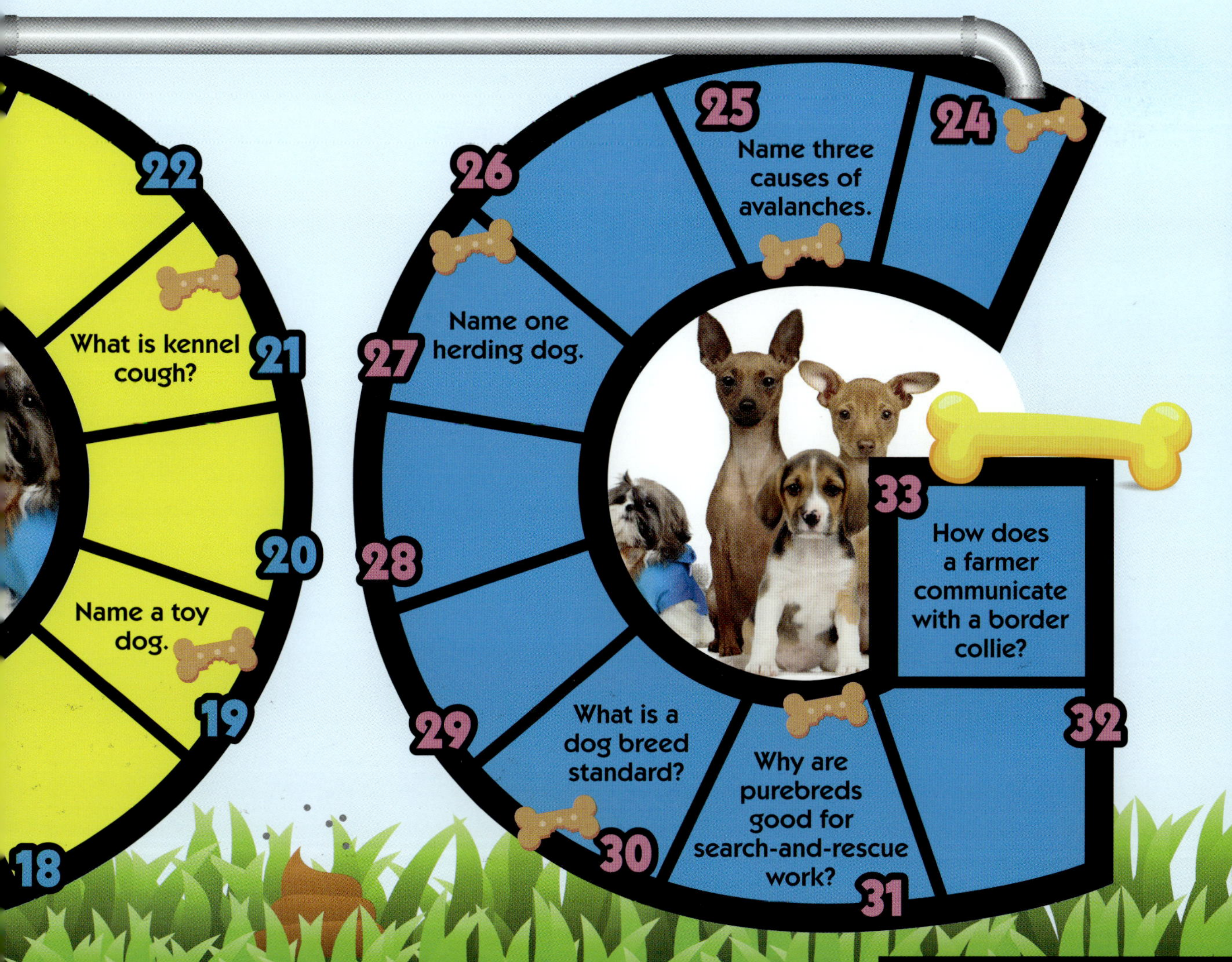

Index

Glossary

disc dog competition A competition that involves dogs attempting to catch round discs in their mouths

dock-diving A sport for dogs whereby each dog is measured on how far it can jump

flyball A team sport for dogs, in which they are required to jump over hurdles and fetch a ball

herding Moving a large number of animals, such as sheep, together as a group. Many dogs are very good at this.

hierarchy A system under which people, or dogs, in a group are ranked in order of importance

olfactory sense The sense of smell

pack A group of dogs that lives and hunts together in the wild

territory An area that a dog feels belongs to it, or its pack. Dogs are usually very protective of their territory.

Dog-Dig-Craft Game Answers

Find the answers for the Dog-Dig-Craft game on the pages listed below:

Game question 1: answer on pages 7–9
Game question 3: answer on page 4
Game question 5: answer on page 15
Game question 8: answer on page 6
Game question 11: answer on page 12
Game question 12: answer on page 13
Game question 14: answer on pages 28–29
Game question 17: answer on page 14
Game question 19: answer on page 18
Game question 21: answer on page 14
Game question 25: answer on page 27
Game question 27: answer on page 16
Game question 30: answer on page 21
Game question 31: answer on page 25
Game question 33: answer on page 22
Bonus Question: answer on page 19